Smelly Dog

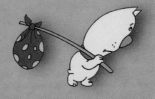

COLLINGWOOD O'HARE ENTERTAINMENT LTD
Created by Trevor Ricketts and Christopher O'Hare
Series developed by Tony Collingwood
Copyright © 2000 by Collingwood O'Hare Entertainment Ltd.

First published in Great Britain in 2000 by HarperCollins*Children's Books*,
a division of HarperCollins*Publishers* Ltd,
77-85 Fulham Palace Road, Hammersmith, London W6 8JB.
ISBN: 0 00 664753 7
1 3 5 7 9 10 8 6 4 2
A CIP catalogue record for this title is available from the British Library.

The HarperCollins website address is:
www.fireandwater.com

Printed and bound in Hong Kong.

ANIMAL
STORIES

Smelly Dog

Written by Trevor Ricketts

Collins
An Imprint of HarperCollinsPublishers

There was a Dog
Who liked to eat
Hot chilli sauce
And spicy meat.

He loved green onions
And mustard spread,
Hot black coffee,
With garlic bread.

The problem was,
That when he spoke,
His breath would pong,
Which made you choke.

"Change your diet!"
His friends would howl,
"Then your breath
Won't smell so foul."

"I can't help it'"
He would say.
"I like my food
The spicy way."

So their advise
He did ignore,
And off he went
To buy some more.

On the way
He met some birds.
He opened his mouth
To say some words.

His nasty breath,
It was a whiff.
They all exclaimed,
"Pooh, what a niff!"

Then later on
He met a cat.
He stopped a while,
Just for a chat.

"How do you do?"
He tried to say,
But the cat fell back,
Knocked out all day.

Poor old Dog.
He felt quite sad.
He didn't think
His breath that bad.

That night he cooked dinner,
With old mushy peas
And rotten tomatoes
In ten week old cheese.

But even at home
People said it was smelly –
And they weren't even there,
They were inside the telly!

His breath it had lost him
Every friend he held dear.
He turned off the TV,
And sniffed back a tear.

Then he got a big sheet,
And packed up his stuff.
He'd leave town at once,
For the woods and live rough.

That way his friends
Could breathe cleaner air.
They'd be happier friends
If he wasn't there.

As he passed by the bank,
He heard a shot and a crash!
Then a Robber ran out
With a bag full of cash.

Alarm bells were ringing,
The cashiers were scared.
Nobody stopped him –
Nobody dared!

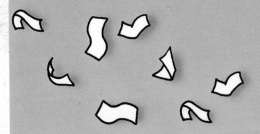

Our Dog did his duty.
He lifted his paw.
He shouted, "Stop Thief!
In the name of the Law!"

Dog's breath hit the Thief,
Like wind from a bellow.
He coughed and he spluttered,
He turned blue and then yellow.

Then he froze on the spot,
And started to lean.
As the thief hit the floor,
His face it turned green.

The Robber had fainted,
Overcome by the pong.
A hero was born!
Dog had righted a wrong!

The Police all arrived
At the scene of the crime.
They arrested the Robber
And said, "You'll do time."

Dog had saved the town.
He had saved the day.
And everyone wanted
Dog to stay.

The bank thanked our hero
And gave him a prize.
His friends all cheered
With tears in their eyes.

But his personal problem
Had not gone away –
Till he opened his prize,
And the crowd shouted
"Hurray!"

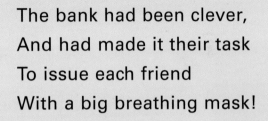

The bank had been clever,
And had made it their task
To issue each friend
With a big breathing mask!

His friends were all pleased,
And so were the bank.
And so was the Dog –
But his breath still stank!

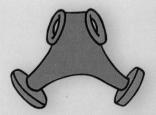

The End